FOR KIT—N. H. F.
FOR RICHARD—V. S.

Text copyright © 2024 by Norman H. Finkelstein
Illustrations copyright © 2024 by Vesper Stamper
All Rights Reserved
HOLIDAY HOUSE is registered in the U.S. Patent and Trademark Office
Printed and bound in October 2023 at Toppan Leefung, DongGuan, China.
The artwork was created in gouache.
www.holidayhouse.com
First Edition
1 3 5 7 9 10 8 6 4 2

Library of Congress Cataloging-in-Publication Data
Names: Finkelstein, Norman H., author. | Stamper, Vesper, illustrator.
Title: Amazing Abe : how Abraham Cahan's newspaper gave a voice to Jewish
immigrants / by Norman H. Finkelstein ; illustrated by Vesper Stamper.
Description: First edition. | New York : Holiday House, 2024. | Includes
bibliographical references. | Audience: Ages 4-8 | Audience: Grades 2-3
Summary: "A tribute to Abraham Cahan, founder of a prominent Yiddish
language newspaper whose discussion of everything from voting rights to
baseball offered crucial guidance to Jewish immigrants"—Provided by publisher.
Identifiers: LCCN 2023028039 | ISBN 9780823451647 (hardcover)
Subjects: LCSH: Cahan, Abraham, 1860-1951—Juvenile literature. | Newspaper
editors—United States—Biography—Juvenile literature. | Yiddish
newspapers—United States—History—Juvenile literature. | Jews—United
States—Intellectual life—Juvenile literature. | LCGFT: Biographies.
Classification: LCC PN4874.C214 F56 2024 | DDC 070.92
[B]—dc23/eng/20230721
LC record available at https://lccn.loc.gov/2023028039

ISBN: 978-0-8234-5164-7 (hardcover)

AMAZING ABE

HOW ABRAHAM CAHAN'S NEWSPAPER GAVE A VOICE TO JEWISH IMMIGRANTS

By Norman H. Finkelstein

Illustrated by Vesper Stamper

HOLIDAY HOUSE • NEW YORK

From a young age, Abe Cahan loved words.

The future newspaperman began his education in the traditional Jewish way, studying Hebrew and the Bible. But that was not enough. Abe wanted to expand his knowledge and began learning Russian language and literature.

But the language he dreamed in was Yiddish.

In the nineteenth century, Lithuania was a part
of the Russian Empire where Jewish people were
permitted to live.

It was called the Pale of Settlement. The language of nearly all Jews in the Pale was Yiddish. And their lives revolved around the Jewish calendar.

Unusual for a Jewish boy of his time, Abe went to college and became
a public school teacher. He also became involved in politics.

At a time when Russians suffered under the rule of the Czars, Abe
actively supported poor and mistreated workers. He made speeches and
distributed anti-government pamphlets knowing that he faced arrest
if caught.

When police came to question him at the school where he taught, he knew his life was in danger. There was no choice. Abe had to leave his homeland at once. Traveling from Russia to Austria to Germany and then to England, he had one goal—to find freedom.

In Liverpool, England, before boarding a ship for the United States, he bought a Russian-English dictionary. During the long journey, he used it to learn English. In New York City, he joined nearly two million other Jews who arrived in the United States from Eastern Europe between 1880 and 1914.

To perfect his English, he got permission from a public school principal to sit in a class with fourteen-year-old middle school students. Abe was twenty-two years old.

Life was not easy. Abe worked in dirty cigar and tin factories by day and continued to study English by night. He then used his language skills to teach English to other immigrants. Having witnessed firsthand the terrible shop conditions that people were forced to work in, Abe also used his way with words to fight for workers' rights.

With his new mastery of English, he began reporting for American newspapers about the experiences of Jewish immigrants. But his first love was still Yiddish. It was the language of his parents' home and the Jewish world that had once surrounded him.

So in 1897, he helped found a
Yiddish newspaper, *Forverts*—known in
English as *The Jewish Daily Forward*. He soon
became the paper's editor. Although his readers came
from many countries, they were united in a common language:
Yiddish. Soon, the *Forverts* became the largest foreign-language
newspaper in the country, with a readership greater than some of
America's leading English-language papers. His newspaper welcomed
everyone, educated and not, rich and poor, young and old.

The *Forverts* kept readers in touch with news from around the world and their neighborhoods. But Abe knew that was not enough.

While Jewish immigrants discovered that America was a land of opportunity, they also discovered that life here would not be easy. New language. New customs. New ways to dress. New ways to think.

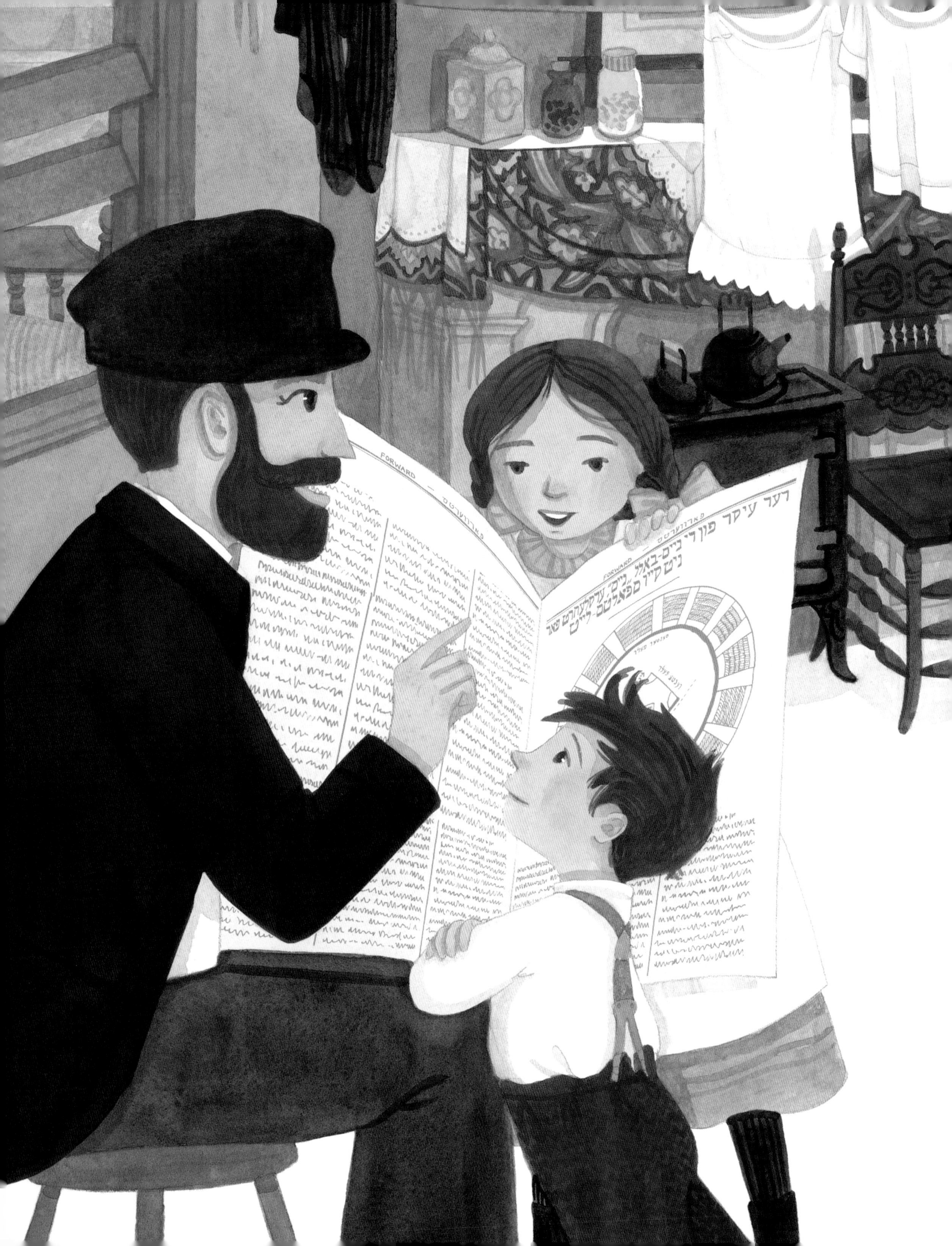
FORWARD
פארווערטס
פארווערטס
FORWARD

Always a teacher, Abe helped them. He explained baseball to his readers, with diagrams and full instructions about how the game was played. He taught them how to set their tables in the American way, describing how the forks, knives, and spoons should be placed. To avoid the spread of germs in cramped tenements, he advised everyone to use handkerchiefs when they sneezed.

Abe taught them about democracy, American history, and the importance of voting. He urged readers to join labor unions to improve their working conditions and pay.

Still, readers worried about everyday personal problems. Getting a job. Feeding their families. Educating their children. Homesickness. Adapting to American life. For help, they turned to Abe. He understood their needs and created a special column, the *Bintel Brief (Bundle of Letters)*, where readers could write in for advice.

And what questions they had!

A fourteen-year-old girl in a large family wrote that she wanted to continue her education but her family was poor and needed her to work. What should she do? Abe's advice: Go to school so you will then get a good job and be of greater help to your family.

A father wrote that he was upset with an older son who played baseball. In Europe, the father explained, a boy of his age would act seriously and not be chasing after a little ball. Abe's advice: As long as baseball doesn't interfere with his studies, let him play. In America, children need to strengthen their bodies and not just their minds.

A woman wrote that she wanted to go to night school twice a week to improve her English. Her husband was opposed. Abe's advice: She had every right to go.

A girl suffering from tuberculosis asked where she could go for a cure and didn't know how she could afford it, and readers responded by sending enough money to help her.

When relatives in Europe lost contact with their families who immigrated to America, Abe published their names in the paper and reunited them.

When readers wanted more than news, Abe published stories by talented Yiddish writers such as Isaac Bashevis Singer. His own books and stories, written in English, introduced American readers to the lives of their new immigrant neighbors. For the rest of his life, through the pages of the *Forverts* and wherever he found an audience, Abe continued to speak up for the rights of immigrants, workers, and the poor.

With the newspaper's success, Abe built a ten-story building with a blazing electric *Forverts* sign in Yiddish on top. That sign and the newspaper he created were beacons of hope to those early Yiddish-speaking immigrants. Decades later, although their children and grandchildren may not speak Yiddish, we remember that it was Abe and his *Forverts* that helped families keep their old traditions while making new lives for themselves in the United States.

31

MORE ABOUT ABE CAHAN

Abraham Cahan was born in Vilnius, Lithuania, on July 7, 1860, into a deeply religious Jewish family. Although his father urged him to become a rabbi, Abe had other ideas. He wanted to be a teacher. In an unusual choice for a Jewish boy, he gained admission to the Vilnius Teacher Training Institute and became a public school teacher. Living in the Russian Empire, he was clearly aware of the poverty, discrimination, and terrible working conditions that surrounded him. He became actively involved in revolutionary activities to overthrow the Czar. With the assassination of Czar Alexander II in 1881, conditions worsened for Jews in the Russian Empire. Violent pogroms and harsh laws deprived Jews of their rights. Abe found himself targeted by the police for his political activism. Fearing for his life, he joined two million other Jews who left Russia behind and arrived in the United States.

In New York City, he became active in labor unions and joined the Socialist Labor Party. He loved languages and became so proficient in English that he worked as a reporter for several New York English-language newspapers. He also began writing English-language novels about the experiences of Jewish immigrants. His first, *Yekl: A Tale of the New York Ghetto,* brought him fame as a writer. His later book, *The Rise of David Levinsky,* published in 1917, remains a literary classic today.

In 1897, he helped create the *Forverts,* the *Jewish Daily Forward,* and became its editor in 1903, holding that position until 1946. Unlike other Jewish newspapers of the time, the *Forverts* was established as a nonprofit institution. The newspaper played an important role in the lives of its readers. A common slogan was "What is a home without the *Forverts?*"

He died on August 31, 1951, at the age of 91, leaving behind the legacy of making Jewish immigrants feel at home in America.

Over decades, as the number of Yiddish readers diminished, so too did the newspaper's circulation. An English-language version began in 1990, and it became an online publication in 2019.

AUTHOR'S NOTE

My relationship with the *Forverts* began at a very young age. My grandparents and parents arrived from Europe with Yiddish as their first language. In America, the *Forverts* was their link to the world. My job was to often pick up the newspaper for them at a local deli. My own Yiddish abilities were minimal, but I was specifically attracted to the Sunday issues, which contained a separate section with sepia news photographs from around the world with English subtitles.

Like many others, I forgot about the *Forverts* until they began publishing an English edition. The political slant of the "new" *Forward* was the same, but the newspaper was made relevant to a new generation of readers who did not know Yiddish.

Coming to a new land is not an easy experience. Abraham Cahan created the path for Jewish immigrants like my grandparents and parents for fulfilling lives in America.

MORE ABOUT YIDDISH

In Eastern Europe, before World War II, the everyday language of most Jewish people was Yiddish. Developed from German, it contains words in Hebrew and from the languages spoken in the countries where Jews lived. It was written in Hebrew letters. Although Jewish people immigrated to the United States from many Eastern European countries at the end of the nineteenth and beginning of the twentieth centuries, it was Yiddish that connected them to each other.

With each passing generation, decreasing numbers spoke it as English became their native language. Today, Yiddish is still used by some ultra-Orthodox Jews as their everyday language. There is a resurgence in interest as many universities offer Yiddish language courses. The Yiddish Book Center in Amherst, Massachusetts (www.yiddishbookcenter.org), preserves Yiddish culture by collecting, translating, and distributing Yiddish books and offering language courses.

TIME LINE

1860	Abraham Cahan born July 7 in Vilnius, Lithuania
1877	Enters the Vilnius Teacher Training Institute
1881	Begins teaching in a Jewish public school in Velizh
1881	Czar Alexander II assassinated
1882	Abe arrives in the United States on June 6
1883	Begins teaching English to immigrants in the Night School of the Young Men's Hebrew Association
1885	Marries Anna Bronstein
1896	Publishes first novel, *Yekl*
1897	Founds the *Forverts*
1912	Lays cornerstone for the new *Forward* building on East Broadway
1917	Publishes *The Rise of David Levinsky*
1951	Abraham Cahan dies on August 29 in New York City

BIBLIOGRAPHY

Cahan, Abraham, et al. *The Education of Abraham Cahan*. Philadelphia: Jewish Publication Society, 1969.

Howe, Irving. *World of Our Fathers*. New York: Schocken, 1989.

Lipsky, Seth. *The Rise of Abraham Cahan*. New York: Schocken, 2013.

Marovitz, Sanford. *Abraham Cahan*. New York: Twyane, 1996.

Metzker, Isaac. *A Bintel Brief*. Garden City, New Jersey: Doubleday, 1971.

Rischin, Moses, ed. *Grandma Never Lived in America*. Bloomington, Indiana: Indiana University Press, 1985.

SUGGESTED READING FOR YOUNG READERS

Levy, Debbie. *Yiddish Saves the Day*. New York: Apples & Honey Press, 2019.

Macy, Sue. *The Book Rescuer: How a Mensch from Massachusetts Saved Yiddish Literature for Generations to Come*. New York: Simon & Schuster, 2019.

Nadler, Jill Ross. *Such a Library: A Yiddish Folktale Re-Imagined*. Seattle: Intergalactic Afikoman, 2020.

Newman, Leslea. *Gittel's Journey: An Ellis Island Story*. New York: Abrams, 2019.

Sussman, Joni. *My First Yiddish Word Book*. Minneapolis: Kar-Ben, 2014.